Annie and Snowball and the Grandmother Night

The Twelfth Book of Their Adventures

Cynthia Rylant

Illustrated by Suçie Stevenson

READY-TO-READ

SIMON SPOTLIGHT

New York   London   Toronto   Sydney   New Delhi

For all the grandmothers
—C. R.

For wonderful grandmas everywhere!
—S. S.

SIMON SPOTLIGHT
An imprint of Simon & Schuster Children's Publishing Division
1230 Avenue of the Americas, New York, New York 10020
Text copyright © 2012 by Cynthia Rylant
Illustrations copyright © 2012 by Suçie Stevenson
SIMON SPOTLIGHT, READY-TO-READ, and colophon are
registered trademarks of Simon & Schuster, Inc.
For information about special discounts for bulk purchases, please contact
Simon & Schuster Special Sales at 1-866-506-1949 or business@simonandschuster.com.
The Simon & Schuster Speakers Bureau can bring authors to your live event. For more
information or to book an event contact the Simon & Schuster Speakers Bureau
at 1-866-248-3049 or visit our website at www.simonspeakers.com.
Designed by Tom Daly
The text of this book was set in Goudy Old Style.
The illustrations for this book were rendered in pen-and-ink and watercolor.
Manufactured in China 0612 SCP
First Simon Spotlight hardcover edition September 2012
2 4 6 8 10 9 7 5 3 1
Library of Congress Cataloging-in-Publication Data
Rylant, Cynthia.
Annie and Snowball and the grandmother night : the twelfth book of their adventures /
by Cynthia Rylant ; illustrated by Suçie Stevenson. — 1st ed.
p. cm. — (Ready-to-read)
Summary: Annie and her pet bunny, Snowball, go to Grandmother's house
for a special sleepover.
[1. Sleepovers—Fiction. 2. Grandmothers—Fiction. 3. Rabbits—Fiction.]
I. Stevenson, Suçie, ill. II. Title.
PZ7.R982Anng 2012
[E]—dc23
2011019948
ISBN 978-1-4169-7203-7 (hardcover : alk. paper)
ISBN 978-1-4169-8253-1 (eBook)

Contents

Someone Special

Annie loved her family.
She loved her aunts and uncles
and cousins (especially Henry!).

She loved her father
and her bunny, Snowball.
(Snowball was family to Annie.)

And someone she loved in a very
special way.
It was her grandmother.

One night every month
Annie stayed at her grandmother's house.
And a grandmother night was . . . tonight!

Annie wanted to pack all
her stuffed animals.

But Annie's dad said that she should
just take two.
Oh dear! Who to take?
Annie chose two little mice.

She promised the other animals
that they would get
a grandmother night too.
They all looked happy about that.

Annie said to Snowball,
"I'm glad you aren't stuffed.
You always get to go!"

Grandmother!

On the drive to Grandmother's house,
Annie read books to her dad.
Her dad liked funny books the best,
so Annie read joke books to him.
They laughed and laughed.
Snowball took a long nap.

When they finally arrived,
Grandmother was standing at her door.

She scooped Annie and
Snowball into her arms.

She was smiling so brightly.
She told Annie that her hair
looked pretty and that she liked
Annie's sparkly shoes.

Grandmother told Snowball
that Snowball was a very good bunny.
She gave Annie's dad a kiss on the cheek.
Then she brought them into her house.

Grandmother had the best house.
It was soft and warm, just like her.

It had soft chairs. It had pretty lamps.

It had a bowl full of peppermints.

It even had a budgie.

The budgie's name was Marty.
Annie loved Marty.
She said hello to him and gave him
a bit of Snowball's apple.

Marty bounced and chirped.
Like Grandmother, he loved company.
Everyone felt so happy.

Just Girls

Annie's dad had a cup of tea,
and then he said good-bye.
"You girls have fun," he said as he left.
"We will!" said Annie and Grandmother.

23

Then they went right to the kitchen.
Baking cookies was always
at the top of their list.

While the cookies baked
they played a game of tic-tac-toe.
Annie called it tic-tac-cookie dough.

25

Later they ate cookies and
watched their favorite movie.
It was about three lost pets
who find their way home.

"If Snowball ever got lost," said Annie,
"Mudge would find her."
Mudge was Cousin Henry's big dog
that Annie loved.

After the movie
Annie and Grandmother
said good night to Marty.
Grandmother put a nice cover
over his cage.

Marty liked to sleep in the dark.

"Sweet dreams, Marty," said Annie.

It was time for bed.

Time to Go

Annie and Grandmother always
did three things before bed.
First they washed up.
Then they braided each other's hair.
Then they told each other a story.

It was always a story from their lives.
Tonight Annie told Grandmother
the story of visiting the zoo
with Cousin Henry's family.

Grandmother told Annie
the story of learning
to ride a horse when she was small.

They loved story time.
They learned a lot about each other,
and the stories always gave them good
dreams.

The next morning Annie's dad
came to take her home.

First they all had blueberry pancakes.

Then they all went for a walk.

Then it was time to go home.

37

Annie thanked her grandmother
for such a nice time.
Grandmother hugged her and told Annie
she loved her.

Then Annie said good-bye to Marty, and
Grandmother said good-bye to Snowball.

"I can't wait to come back again,"
said Annie. She got in the car
and waved and waved
to Grandmother.

"How was your night?" asked Annie's dad.

Annie smiled.

"Just perfect," she said.